It Couldn't Be Worse!

by Vlasta van Kampen

 **Annick Press**

Toronto + New York + Vancouver

We acknowledge the support of the Canada Council for the Arts, the Ontario Arts Council, and the Government of Canada through the Book Publishing Industry Development Program (BPIDP) for our publishing activities.

Cataloging in Publication Data

Van Kampen, Vlasta
    It couldn't be worse! / written and illustrated by Vlasta van Kampen.

ISBN 1-55037-783-3 (bound).—ISBN 1-55037-782-5 (pbk.)

1. Picture books for children. I. Title.

PS8593.A56I8 2003   jC813'.54   C2002-902494-3
PZ7

The art in this book was rendered in watercolor.

Distributed in Canada by:
Firefly Books Ltd.
3680 Victoria Park Avenue
Willowdale, ON
M2H 3K1

Published in the U.S.A. by Annick Press (U.S.) Ltd.
Distributed in the U.S.A. by:
Firefly Books (U.S.) Inc.
P.O. Box 1338
Ellicott Station
Buffalo, NY 14205

Manufactured in China

visit us at: www.annickpress.com

For Barbara van Kampen, my wise niece in the Netherlands.
    "Goede raad is duur"
        Good advice is precious
            —V.v.K.

Other Annick Press titles by Vlasta van Kampen
Bear Tales
A Drop of Gold

The tiny house had just one room.

A poor farmer, his wife, their six children, and the grandparents lived there.

They quarreled and fought and got in each other's way.

One day the farmer's wife went to buy fish at the market. The old fish-monger politely asked about her family. She told him of their unhappy situation: the noise, the quarreling, the fighting! **It couldn't be worse.**

The old fishmonger asked her if they had any animals.
When she told him that they had

a goat,

a sheep,

a pig,

a rooster,

some chickens,

and a cow,

he advised her to take the goat into the house.
Then things would get better.

The woman was dumbfounded by this strange advice. Take that unruly goat into their tiny house? But hadn't the fishmonger sailed the seven seas and from all of his adventures gathered wisdom in such matters? He was such a wise man.

The woman returned home. When she told her husband what the fishmonger had said, he shook his head in disbelief.

But it was decided that they would follow his advice. He was such a wise man.

So they untied their goat and hustled him into the house.

The very next day the poor woman returned to the fishmonger.

She told him that things couldn't be worse!

The fishmonger smiled and told her to take their sheep into the house. Then things would get better.

As the woman and her husband pushed and pulled and finally got the sheep into the house, they could only agree that the fishmonger was such a wise man.

The next day the frazzled woman hurried back to the fishmonger.

She told him that things couldn't be worse!

The fishmonger nodded wisely and told her to take their pig into the house. Then things would get better.

The woman was soon home, and she and her husband prodded and nudged the pig into the house. The family all agreed that the fishmonger must be such a wise man.

The next day the frustrated woman was back at the fishmonger's stall.

She told him that things couldn't be worse!

The fishmonger suggested they take their rooster and chickens into the house. Then things would get better.

Back home, the woman and her husband hurried and scurried the chickens into the house. They could only follow the advice of someone who was such a wise man.

The next day the agitated woman arrived at the fishmonger's.

She told him that things couldn't be worse!

The fishmonger smiled and told her to take their cow into the house. Then things would get better.

She dashed home, and this time the whole family shoved and tugged and finally got the cow into the house.

They were amazed that there was still room for her, which only showed what a wise man the fishmonger was.

The next day the desperate woman returned to the fishmonger. She burst into tears.

She told him that things couldn't be worse!

The fishmonger smiled broadly and told her that she should take all of the animals out of the house. Then things would definitely get better.

The woman ran all the way home. Now they herded all of the animals out of the house. The fishmonger had all the answers. He was clearly such a wise man.

A few days later the woman returned to the market to buy some fish. When the old fishmonger asked how her family was, she told him that things couldn't be better.

With all of the animals out, there was **no** quarreling, **no** fighting, and **plenty** of room for everyone.

It was much better than before!

After all, the fishmonger was such a wise man.